WEEKLY READER CHILDREN'S BOOK CLUB

EDUCATION CENTER • COLUMBUS, OHIO 43216

Long Lonesome Train Whistle

BOOKS BY VIRGINIA H. ORMSBY

Long Lonesome Train Whistle
Cunning is Better than Strong
The Little Country Schoolhouse
Twenty-one Children
It's Saturday
Here We Go

WEEKLY READER CHILDREN'S BOOK CLUB

Presents

Long Lonesome

Train Whistle

BY VIRGINIA H. ORMSBY

Illustrated by the Author

J. B. Lippincott Company

PHILADELPHIA • NEW YORK

For my aunt, Mary L. Inman,
with love and appreciation.

Contents

Long Lonesome Train Whistle

CHAPTER 1.

Long Lonesome Train Whistle

Lee lived in the country down in Georgia, a long time ago. He lived with his father and mother and his sister Maggie Ellen, and Bubber, his little brother, and his new baby sister Ruby Pearl, and his dog named Pomp.

Lee was ten, going on eleven, and he was a big boy for his age.

His mother said, "Pretty soon I'll have to be a-cutting your pa's clothes down to fit you. I can't seem to keep you in jeans."

And his pa said, "Lee takes after my granddaddy, with them big old long legs of his. Why, my granddaddy could outrun a mule, they say."

Lee's brown eyes would twinkle and his freckles would almost dance across his nose and he would laugh and say, "Anybody could outrun our old mule. I can walk faster than he can trot."

Lee loved his folks and his dog and his house with its two chimneys to keep it warm in winter, and its two porches and the chinaberry umbrella tree to keep it cool in summer. He loved to sit in the dark on soft summer nights and listen to his father's fiddle and hear the tree frogs singing and the katydids talking back and forth to each other in the treetops. He loved to hear the creaking song of his mother's chair as she rocked Ruby Pearl to sleep and Bubber's soft laugh when Maggie Ellen tickled his fat neck. But most of all he loved the call of the long, lonesome train whistle that blew across the valley.

"Oooooooooo-Weeeeeeeee-Ooooooooo," it sang in the distance. "Oooooo-Weeeeee-Ooooooo."

It filled Lee with longing and he would say to his pa, "Where you reckon that old train is a-going this time of night?"

And his pa would say, "That sounds like a freight train away over in Sugar Valley. She might be pulling a hundred cars or more."

Sometimes, when the wind was just right, Lee could hear a train climbing the grade over Chinquapin Hill. Just after dark on a long summer night, she would climb the hill, all out of breath.

"Chuff - chuff - chuff - chuff - CHUFF - CHUFF - CHUFF - CHUFF - chuff - chuff - chuff - chuff - CHUFF - CHUFF - CHUFF - CHUFF," she panted.

And Lee would say, "That's the passenger train that's a-heading for Atlanta. Along about noon tomorrow she'll turn around and go back to Chattanooga."

As soon as the train got over the top of Chinquapin Hill and down into Sugar Valley she'd seem to hum a little tune that said, "At-LAN-ta, At-LAN-ta, At-LAN-ta." And then she'd call back over her shoulder, "Ooooo-Weeeee-Ooooo, Ooooo-Weeeee-Ooooo."

Pomp would raise his head up off his paws and answer in a mournful howl, and Lee would say, "One of these days I'm a-going to Atlanta and when I'm grown I'm a-going to be a engineer and run one of them old big steam engines."

Then his ma would creak her rocking chair back and forth on the floorboards and hug Ruby Pearl up close to her and say, "Railroading is mighty dangerous. Why, you couldn't pay me just to *ride* on a train."

And Maggie Ellen would cuddle Bubber up close to her and say, "Me and Bubber might ride on a train when Bubber gets

big. But I'd sure be a-scared to go over that old shaky trestle at Nickajack Creek. The train might run plumb off it." And she shivered a little just thinking about it.

Then Pa would say, "My uncle Tom Henderson was a railroad man for nigh onto fifty year and he like to got kilt more than once." And Pa would sit quietly, remembering. "Old Uncle Tom was in a head-on collision one time and he jumped just in the nick of time. But that didn't stop him from railroading."

Lee and Maggie Ellen wished their pa would tell about his uncle Tom's wreck. It made shivers run down their spines when he told about the two speeding trains meeting on the same track on a black winter's night. But they knew it took a roaring hickory fire and a howling wind outside to put Pa in a story-telling mood. Instead, he scraped his fiddle bow across the strings of his fiddle to get in tune and patted his foot and sang, in his deep voice that had a tremble in it:

> Many a man's been murdered by the railroad,
>   railroad, railroad,
> Many a man's been murdered by the railroad,
>   railroad, railroad,
> And laid in his lonesome grave.

Then Pa would stand up and stretch and say, "Well, I reckon we'd all better fly up. It's a-getting late. Bubber and Ruby Pearl are asleep already."

Long after everyone else was asleep Lee would lie awake

listening for the lonesome train whistle. Maybe the freight train with the hundred cars would be coming back from its trip across Sugar Valley. Maybe another train would climb over Chinquapin Hill on its way to Atlanta. Lee tried to imagine what it would be like to ride on a train and go to a big city like Atlanta. But he always fell asleep before he could picture it.

In the daytime the train whistle didn't sound quite so lonesome. Sometimes it had a busy, jolly sound as it hurried across Sugar Valley on its way back to Chattanooga.

"Tooooooot-Tooooooot-Toot-Toot," it called, as it climbed the grade over Chinquapin Hill. And the train wheels sang a merry song after they crossed the wooden trestle over Nickajack Creek.

"CHATTA-noo-ga, CHATTA-noo-ga, CHATTA-noo-ga, CHATTA-noo-ga," they hummed contentedly, telling where they were going.

Lee always stopped his work to listen and once when he was hoeing in the cornfield with his pa he said, "Reckon how much would it cost to ride on a train?"

Pa leaned on his hoe and pulled a long stem of grass to chew on and looked at Lee with his twinkling brown eyes.

"It'd cost you a heap." Then he studied Lee for a while and said, "How come you want to ride on a train so bad? I thought you was a homebody."

Then Lee would get a faraway look in his eyes and he'd answer, "That old train whistle makes me want to go places."

Long after the train was out of earshot Lee would stand and

dream about how it would feel to drive the big black steam engine down the hard steel tracks, faster than the wind, with the whistle blowing all the way. He had had a close look at the engine from a great rock that jutted out over the railroad cut on Chinquapin Hill, and he had never forgotten the glimpse he had had of the yawning, red firebox with the fireman shoveling coal into it. The engineer had been almost close enough for Lee to touch his big gloved hand, and he had waved as the train rumbled by. After that Lee had longed to ride on an engine and more than ever he wanted to go to the city.

Lee's folks had never been beyond the sleepy country town of Locust Grove where they went sometimes on a Saturday to buy provisions. But old man Zack, who owned the grist mill where Lee's folks got their corn ground, had been to the city once and had told Lee all about it.

"Why, they's big buildings all stuck together on both sides of the street and they's not a blade of grass anywhere," he had said. "And folks is all over everwhere, thick as flies on a honeypot."

And Aunt Susan, who was their closest neighbor, knew all about Atlanta and could talk about it for hours once she got started.

"My mammy was a slave and she lived in Atlanta during the Civil War," she would tell Lee. "Why, she was there when Sherman come through on his march to the sea and burned everthing plumb down to the ground. The flames was so high you could see Stone Mountain plain as day. And they was heaps

and piles of dead soldiers all around, Yankees and Confederates both."

After that Lee made up his mind that, somehow, he would get enough money to go to Atlanta. And he would see the mountain made of nothing but one big stone. And maybe he might even see some Yankees. Lee knew what the Confederates were because his father's folks had fought with General Lee, and that was where Lee had got his name. But he couldn't picture a Yankee to save his soul.

Then his father had said, "Yankees are folks same as the rest of us." And Lee had been surprised.

One evening after supper Lee said to his ma, "Reckon I could have some eggs to sell in town? Our old big dominecker hen has got a nest off in the woods somewhere and maybe I could find it."

But his mother had said, "I need my egg money. Ever egg you could scratch up means something to me."

And when Lee had asked his pa if he could keep some of the money for helping cut the cordwood his father sometimes sold in town, Pa had replied, "I need ever bit of cash money I can lay my hands on to buy provisions." And then he had thought a minute and had said, "How come you don't go over towards Chinquapin Hill and pick some blackberries? They ought to be getting ripe along about now, and folks in town will buy them, sure."

So Lee had made up his mind then and there that he would go the next day and pick berries.

CHAPTER 2.

Yankee Prisoners

Lee helped his father extra well next morning and brought in plenty of stovewood for his mother and fetched some good cold water from the spring. Then he found a bucket for the berries and whistled for Pomp and they set off together down the pink dusty lane that went to the big red road.

The vines and hedges along the lane were filled with insect songs and a catbird mewed and scolded as Pomp bounded in an out among the bushes. A line of partridges crossed Lee's path and disappeared with a sudden whirring of wings as he came near.

Across the big red road was another road, crooked and deep-rutted, that led past the Cash farm and on to Chinquapin Hill.

Maybe I can get one of the Cash boys to go berry-picking with me, Lee thought, wishing he had some company.

There was always plenty of company to be had at the Cashes because every year there was a new baby and now there were ten children. They were every one blue-eyed and tow-headed, and to Lee they all looked exactly alike, except for size.

When he turned in at the Cash place five or six lean, hungry-looking hounds came bounding out from under the house and surrounded Pomp, bellowing at him in their hollow voices. Pomp stood growling deep in his throat, with his tail curved stiffly over his back and his eyes rolled until the whites showed. He stood his ground until one by one the Cash dogs wandered back under the house and sat down with a sigh, watching Pomp with sorrowful brown eyes.

Lee called out, "Hey, anybody home?" and suddenly Jaycee, the ten-year-old Cash boy, came galloping around the house followed by three younger brothers, who were waving sticks and grabbing at Jaycee's shirt-tail.

Jaycee turned to his little brothers when he saw Lee. "You all wait now while I talk with General Lee here. You can't capture me now 'cause I'm on the Confederate side. You all run see can you catch another spy."

"What kind of game you all think you a-playing, anyway?" Lee wanted to know.

"I'm a-minding Roy and Loy and Stonewall Jackson," Jaycee

explained, "and we're a-playing Yankee Prisoners."

"Where's the rest of your brothers and sisters at?" Lee asked. "They's usually a whole mess of kids around your place."

"They all gone to town in the wagon with Ma and Pa," Jaycee said. "They wasn't room for me and Stonewall Jackson and the twins, so I'm a-minding them. We're a-playing Yankees and Confederates. I'm a spy and they're a-trying to take me prisoner."

"Reckon you could go blackberry picking with me over to Chinquapin Hill?" Lee asked. "Couldn't nothing happen to your brothers anyway. It's just a little piece across the pasture."

Jaycee tucked in his shirt-tail and thought a minute. Across the yard Roy and Loy and Stonewall Jackson were happily chasing the ducks and chickens and screaming, "Yonder goes some Yankee soldiers. Head 'em off!"

"We might see the train," Lee urged. "I know where there's a big rock where you can see it good."

Suddenly Jaycee made up his mind. He called out to his brothers, "You all see how many prisoners you can catch time I get back. Me and General Lee are a-going to inspect the troops over on Chinquapin Hill."

Across the road from the Cash place a meadow stretched away beyond a fence which sagged under tangles of honeysuckle and blackberry vines. Lee and Jaycee looked for the ripe berries, which were fat and black and came off easily from their stems.

"Hope we don't run up on no rattlesnakes," Jaycee worried. "Liable to be a heap of 'em under these vines."

But Lee was anxious to fill his bucket. "There's a-plenty of blackberry vines along the railroad cut," he said. "Let's go on over there and see can we find some more berries."

A wandering cowpath led across the meadow to the woods on Chinquapin Hill and the boys climbed the crooked-rail fence and set out along the path. Some cows looked up from their grazing and watched with soft, peaceful eyes, chewing lazily. As Jaycee passed the cows he licked the first finger of his right hand and pressed it into the palm of his left hand and stamped his

palm with his right fist. Then he turned around twice and spit in his tracks.

"What you think you're a-doing?" Lee wanted to know.

"I'm a-marking out the cows," Jaycee said. "It's bad luck to pass a four-footed critter 'lessen you mark him out."

"I must be unlucky then," Lee laughed, " 'cause I sure have passed a heap of four-footed critters in my life and I never marked a one of them out yet."

Pomp squeezed under the fence and bounded ahead of the boys, then changed his mind and came back to worry the cows and nip at their heels. A rabbit darted out of the honeysuckle vines and streaked across the pasture, and Pomp followed barking frantically. The rabbit doubled back and popped under the fence and crossed the road toward the Cash place. Pomp disappeared from view and Lee said, "That rabbit is long gone, but Pomp'll chase after him anyway."

Chinquapin Hill was thickly wooded with oaks and hickories and the chinquapin bushes that gave the hill its name. Jaycee found a patch of cool green moss and threw himself down on it. "Let's us set a spell," he said. "I'm plumb wore out."

But Lee said, "We better get them berries along the railroad bank before the train comes."

A faint path wandered through the woods and led the boys gently downhill until they reached the railroad tracks. Here the berries were thicker and the boys picked and picked until Lee's bucket was nearly full.

"Let's us stop and rest," Jaycee said. "Them old blackberry vines is too scratchy."

But Lee said, "There's a heap more berries across the tracks. I wish I had me another bucket."

"I wouldn't be caught dead in them woods acrost the tracks," Jaycee said. "They's wild hogs over there and they's a old crazy woman that lives in a haunted house and she done put a spell on them old hogs."

Lee looked at the path that wound its way into the woods and said, "How come you know so much about it?" And he still wished he had brought another bucket for the berries.

"Me and Roy and Loy and Stonewall Jackson was over that-a-way once," Jaycee told him, "and we run up on them hogs and one of them knocked Loy down and like to wallowed him to death."

Lee knew that a hog could be dangerous, especially a sow with a litter of pigs. Many a time he had been cautioned by his parents to see that Bubber didn't wander off alone to the hog pen. Still he didn't believe there were wild hogs in the woods across the track or, if there were, that anyone had put a spell on them.

"How come you think a old crazy woman lives over there?" he asked Jaycee. "You ever see her?"

"We all seen her," Jaycee insisted. "They's a old graveyard and a burnt-down house with just the chimbley a-sticking up and then you come to Crazy Sara's house. They's real ghostie music and a funny kind of crying that comes out of her house when you pass it. And when the hogs was after us she come out and screeched bloody-murder!"

Lee remembered the time last year when he had been scared out of a year's growth when he went alone to the swamp and thought he was being chased by the Whankos his father had told about and how he had really believed there were one-eyed humans that lived in the swamp. He laughed.

"I'll believe it when I see it," he said. "I got a notion to go over there this minute and see for myself."

But, just then, from far off in the distance came the long, lonesome call of a train whistle.

"Hurry!" Lee said, grabbing up the bucket of berries. "Yonder comes the train!"

The boys just had time to scramble up the railroad embankment and run along its top until they came to a large overhanging rock that jutted out of the raw red clay of the cut. Almost before they could settle themselves the great black engine appeared around the curve, billowing smoke and steam and snaking its coaches behind it like a monster with a long waving tail.

"Yonder she comes!" Lee said, under his breath, trying not to show his excitement.

"CHATTA-noo-ga, CHATTA-noo-ga, CHATTA-noo-ga, CHATTA-noo-ga," chuffed the engine, and away down the road the engineer stuck his head out of the cab window and began to wave at the boys. As the engine neared, he pulled the whistle in a long "hello!"

Lee was almost close enough to reach out and touch the engineer. He could see his broad smiling face and his twinkling blue eyes and the red bandanna handkerchief around his neck. The engineer and fireman laughed and nodded, waved some more, and then they were gone. But Lee had time to memorize the big brass numbers on the side of the engine before it had pulled the last of its coaches over Chinquapin Hill.

"Thirteen-twenty-six," he said. "I'll know that number next time I see it."

"That's a unlucky number," Jaycee warned. "Thirteen is unlucky and two thirteens is twenty-six, and that's double trouble."

"Well, if 1326 is unlucky," Lee said, "I wisht I could be unlucky enough to ride on that engine just once. I'd be long gone by now."

CHAPTER 3.

Double Trouble

The Cash place looked strangely deserted when Lee and Jaycee came back from Chinquapin Hill. Not a child was in sight, and even the chickens and ducks had disappeared from the yard. The doors and the shutters of the house were tightly closed, and even the hounds were gone. Jaycee broke into a run and called back to Lee, "I'll get whupped, sure, if Roy and Loy and Stonewall Jackson has got into mischief."

When Lee caught up with Jaycee he was pushing hard against the front door trying to get in and a voice that sounded like Stonewall Jackson's yelled, "Give the password! This here is the guardhouse and we got it full of Yankee prisoners." The voice was drowned out by the sounds of furniture being knocked over and by the squeals of Roy and Loy and a loud mournful barking somewhere in the back.

"Stonewall Jackson Cash, you open this door 'fore I whup the tar out of you!" Jaycee ordered, and the door was opened just wide enough for Jaycee and Lee to squeeze inside. Lee set his bucket of berries near the door and tried to get used to the darkness inside the house.

"We got fifteen Yankee prisoners," Roy and Loy shouted, both together, "and they's a sure enough spy in the cookshed."

"We like to never caught him," said Stonewall Jackson. "He come streaking across the road when you all went to Chinquapin Hill and we headed him off."

"Shut the door, quick!" screamed Roy and Loy. "Don't let 'em get out!"

Lee squinted his eyes trying hard to see into the shadows of the darkened room. There was something lumpish staggering helplessly about in the middle of one of the featherbeds, and a line of chickens wandered about the room craning their necks and flapping their wings in an effort to escape.

"You all are sure a-going to get skinned when your ma gets home," Lee said.

But Jaycee was yelling frantically to his brothers, "I never meant for you all to catch them sure enough. It was only a game we was a-playing!"

The barking in the cookshed became wilder, and five or six

ducks flapped and stumbled across the room quacking loudly.

"Hey," Lee shouted, "that sounds like old Pomp a-barking in there." And he started for the cookshed door.

"Don't let him out!" screamed Stonewall Jackson. "That's the spy. It took all three of us to capture him." But by now Lee had the door open and Pomp darted out like a streak of lightning and raced madly around the room looking for a way out.

Lee made a dash for the front door, calling, "Here, Pomp! Here, boy!" But he stumbled over Roy and Loy and fell across the bed. The lumpish shape suddenly came alive with ear-splitting squeals and scrambled to the floor.

"A pig!" Lee shouted, not believing his eyes. "You all are sure gonna get skinned when your ma finds out!"

But nobody heard him over the din. Jaycee was trying to head off the pig, which was knocking about crazily, overturning chairs and sending the ducks and chickens into a mad, flurrying flight.

Stonewall Jackson and Roy and Loy were screaming, "Don't let him get away!" and "Here he comes!" and "He's under the bed!" and "There he goes!" and "He's a-heading for the cook-shed!"

Jaycee was beginning to recover his senses and he called to Lee, "You sic Pomp on him and I'll hold the front door open and we'll run him out that-a-way. Can't nobody catch a fool pig."

Lee called, "Sic him, Pomp! Get him, boy!" And over the wails and protests of the twins and Stonewall Jackson, Pomp went after the pig in the cookshed while Jaycee held open the front door.

There was a terrific clatter of pots and pans and scattered stovewood and, amid squeals and barks and howls and growls, the pig popped out the door of the cookshed with Pomp at his heels. He streaked across the room towards the open door, knocking the twins into a spin and squeezing between the legs of Stonewall Jackson. Too late, Lee remembered the bucket of berries by the door, and all he could say was, "Hey! Look out," when the pig knocked it sky high and sent the berries scattering in every direction.

DOUBLE TROUBLE

Lee didn't bother with the berries. It wasn't any use. The twins and Stonewall Jackson plowed them into a pulp in their pursuit of the pig and Pomp, and the chickens and ducks gobbled up the rest. Lee picked up his empty bucket and left.

"Maybe I should of marked out them four-footed critters and I wouldn't of had bad luck," he said to himself. But then he thought of Jaycee. "He marked them out, though, and he's got worser luck than I have."

Lee could picture what would happen when Jaycee's folks got back from town. He felt bad that he hadn't stayed to help him clean up the mess, but all he could think about now was getting home where it was quiet and peaceful. He hurried after Pomp, and the empty bucket banged sadly against his leg as he walked. But Lee made up his mind to one thing. Tomorrow, he promised himself, I'm a-going across the railroad tracks and pick them berries over near Crazy Sara's, hogs or no hogs. And this time I'm a-going by myself.

CHAPTER 4.

Crazy Sara

Lee was glad the next day that he hadn't asked Jaycee to come with him. He liked being alone with only Pomp for company. He picked blackberries until his hands were stained purple with the juice, and he ate the ripest ones until his tongue was black.

The sun blazed down brightly and the railroad tracks stretched out in either direction, silent and shimmering in the heat. The railroad embankment rose high on both sides of the track as far as the eye could see, in great tree-topped scallops of red clay, or tangled green where vines had grown.

Lee walked the crossties, and liked their warm and splintery feel under his bare feet. Then he walked the hot, silvery rails, balancing himself with waving arms. He wished he could follow the rails as far as they went, but then he thought of the trestle over Nickajack Creek.

What if a train was to come along when I was walking the trestle, and I couldn't get across? he thought, and he pictured himself hanging by his hands from a crosstie over the swirling muddy water while a giant black engine pulled a hundred cars over his head. And he shivered with delight at the danger he imagined!

Pomp had gone ahead on business of his own, and Lee could hear him barking off in the woods in the direction of Crazy Sara's. Maybe Pomp's run up on them wild hogs, Lee thought, if there *is* any such of a thing.

He picked up his half-filled bucket and clambered up the path that lay nearly hidden across the railroad tracks.

The path widened up the hill and led Lee on through the woods and down a shady slope. A light breeze ruffled the leaves at the top of the trees. Lee thought he could make out faded wagon ruts overgrown with grass, and he saw that he was on an old un-used road. Ahead of him the road curved out of sight and he thought, if I keep on to the end of the road I might run up on Pomp or the hogs, one.

Suddenly, around the curve in the road Lee came upon a clearing, and his heart skipped a beat. There before him, stood the chimney of a burnt-down house. The words of the Cash boys came back to him: "They's a chimbley of a old burnt-down house and then they's a graveyard and then you come to Crazy Sara's."

And, "Her house is haunted and they's funny kind of singing coming out of it and real ghostie music!"

The chimney stood gaunt and bare against the sky. Two blackened fireplaces gaped blindly, one at the bottom and one at the top where an upstairs once had been. An apple tree, gnarled and leafless, stood nearby, its branches reaching out hopelessly.

Suddenly Lee noticed that the sky was becoming gray as clouds scudded across the sun. A rain crow called raucously from the woods and faraway thunder rumbled, coming closer. Raindrops, making spots the size of silver dollars, fell one at a time and then faster, touching every leaf in the woods. Lee took shelter under a tree and waited for the shower to stop. The chimney watched him from across the road like a sad, gray ghost.

Pomp's voice sounded close one minute and far off the next, as if he were circling the woods on the trail of something. Lee called, "Here, Pomp! H-e-r-e, Pomp!" But the crackling sound of lightning nearby and a deafening crash of thunder drowned out his voice.

That lightning was mighty close, Lee thought, and he wished he could find something safer than a tree for shelter. Now the rain came down in angry sheets and a sudden spear of lightning flashed, with thunder following it so quickly that Lee raced headlong into the rain and down the road.

Another splintering crackle of lightning and an instant roar of thunder sent him plunging headlong into a clearing where tall

weeds and grasses bent under the rain. Before him he could make
out some dim, gray shapes, like figures standing still and huddled
in the storm.

Suddenly his foot caught on a tangle of vines and he was
thrown flat to the ground and his shoulder struck against something hard. Lee picked himself up and what he saw before him
sent shivers down his spine. The "something hard" was a figure
with arms outstretched and a fat, smiling face with wide-open
eyes and large, unfurled wings over its shoulders. For one ter-
rible second, Lee thought he had been struck by lightning and
had gone to heaven. He moved his hand to see whether he was
still alive, and his hands touched the figure's hand. It was cold
and made of stone. Then Lee knew where he was. It was the
graveyard, and this was a stone angel over one of the graves!

All that Lee remembered afterwards was that he had run and run and run, and that he had kept telling himself, "If I'm a-going to be struck by lightning, it's not a-going to be in no burying-ground."

Suddenly, out of the blinding rain, a dark shape loomed up and Lee saw with relief that it was a house. He dashed up on the rickety front porch, threw himself against the door and crouched on his heels, panting and wringing water out of his clothes. Now that he was safe from the storm he felt a little foolish for having been so scared in the graveyard. Why, he had passed many a burying-ground, even at night, and he hadn't been afraid. This time he had just been startled to meet up with an angel in the middle of a rainstorm. Lee had pretty much gotten over being afraid a long time ago, when he was younger. He didn't have any crazy notions like the Cash kids.

The rain settled down to a steady drumming and now the thunder seemed farther away. Lee thought he could hear Pomp howling, off in the woods somewhere. He listened intently, but what he heard was certainly not a dog's howl. It was something close by—very close—and it sounded like singing and real ghostie music. Lee wanted to laugh, but he felt prickles on the back of his neck in spite of himself. Reckon this was Crazy Sara's house? he thought to himself. Again he thought of Jaycee's words: "First you come to a burnt-down house and then you pass a grave-yard and then you come to Crazy Sara's."

Suddenly the music stopped and there was silence, and then a creaking sound as the door back of him opened. A wrinkled face with faded blue eyes and very few teeth peered down at him, and a woman's high quavery voice said, "You're not one of them boys that was here the other day, are you?"

Lee scrambled to his feet, thinking, I'd better get away from here while the getting's good. But all he said was, "No ma'am. I just come up on the porch to get in out of the rain." And he made a move to go.

The old woman's bony hand grabbed hold of his shoulder and she said, "You can't go like that. You just come here!"

Lee tried to remember what it was that Jaycee always did to mark out danger, but the old woman was half leading and half pushing him over to the fireplace inside her house, where a small fire sighed and sang to itself.

"You're as wet as a bullfrog!" she said. "If you don't dry off some you're liable to catch the croup." And, from the next thing she said, Lee knew the old woman must be Crazy Sara. "I wouldn't of had no part of you if I'd a-thought you was one of them boys that come by here a while back and run off my hogs."

"Was they tow-headed, and two of them just alike?" Lee asked, now that he had found his voice.

"That's them! They was four of them in all," Sara said. "One about your size and a fat, kinda bow-legged boy and two little bitty ones that was the spittin' image of each other."

"Them's the Cash kids," Lee said. "They live over across Chinquapin Hill."

"Well, them two least ones let my hogs out of the pen and when I come out to warn them, they run. Them old hogs of mine is dangerous around strangers," old Sara said. "Why, they wallowed one of them little fellers right down in the ground 'fore I could get across the yard."

Suddenly everything fell into place for Lee. The story Jaycee had told him was true, only Jaycee had told it hindside before. The twins had let the hogs out, and Crazy Sara had had a good reason to come out of her house a-screeching. There wasn't a spell on the hogs and they weren't wild, either. But old Sara knew they were mean and she was only trying to warn the boys.

But what about the music and the funny kind of hollering? Jaycee had told the truth about that, because Lee had heard it himself just a few minutes ago. He looked about the room while Crazy Sara fetched wood to build up the fire. There wasn't much furniture, just a bed, a table and two split-bottom chairs and the rocker by the fireplace where Lee was sitting. And then Lee saw it in the corner by the window—there stood a little organ. It was prettily carved, and a hymn book stood open as if someone had just been playing a song.

"Is that a organ over yonder?" Lee asked politely when Crazy Sara came back.

The old woman smiled and her eyes lit up. She went over to the organ and stroked it lovingly with her gnarled hands.

"This is my pride and joy," she said. "Why, if I didn't have this little old organ to play when I'm lonesome or a-scared I'd go plumb, raving crazy and that's a fact! It surely is!"

Then she sat down and turned a page in the hymn book, and started to pump the organ with her feet and began to sing in her high, cracked voice.

> Shall we gather at the river,
> Where bright angel feet have trod . . .

It was a tune that Lee himself had sung many a time at church, and it was one of his favorites. As he watched Crazy Sara pumping the pedals with her whole body to make the organ play, and singing with all her heart, Lee knew she wasn't crazy at all. She was just a lonesome old woman.

The thunder rumbled in the distance like an angry giant running away and suddenly the sun came out and old Sara got up and opened the front door. All at once Lee heard Pomp's voice baying, frantic and excited, quite near now.

"Roo-roo-roo-roo-ro-o-o-o-o!" he howled. "Roo-roo-roo-roo-ro-o-o-o-o!" Lee jumped to his feet. "That's my dog a-raising Cain out there!" he said. "Reckon he might of run up on your hogs?"

The old woman didn't lose any time. "Well, for the land's sake let's go and see!" she said, and Lee had a hard time keeping up with her as she strode across the yard toward the woods.

Pomp's voice grew louder and nearer. Lee and old Sara pushed through tangles of muscadine vines and low-hanging branches. Suddenly they came to a clearing in the woods and there they found Pomp holding at bay two of the meanest-looking hogs Lee

had ever seen. Pomp was running from one to the other, getting as close as he dared and barking wildly. The hogs stood as if ready to charge, with their heads lowered and their eyes gleaming redly.

Lee watched, holding his breath. Suddenly the old woman's voice shrilled, "Soo, pig! Soo, pig! So-o-o pig!"

Startled, the hogs looked in the direction of the new sound and crashed crazily through the bushes toward Lee and old Sara. Lee jumped, but Sara turned on her heel and started back to the house, still calling, "Soo, pig! Soo, pig!" The pigs followed her, grunting and squealing and twitching their curly tails.

[40]

"You all keep in behind them," Sara called back over her shoulder. "Keep them headed this-a-way. I reckon the poor things is hungry."

Pomp stayed behind the hogs at a safe distance, nudging them now and then with his nose and jumping back when they turned their heads. Lee pulled a switch from a bush and flicked them lightly when they veered off in a different direction. But when Sara reached the hog-pen in the back of her yard and held open the gate calling softly, "Soo, pig! Soo, pig!" they trotted happily into the enclosure and stuck their snouts through the rails of the pen as if to beg old Sara for their supper.

"I'm a-going to pay you for helping me catch my hogs," Sara said after she had brought out a big bucket of scraps for the pigs.

But Lee said, "I didn't do nothing. I couldn't take no money for what I did."

But old Sara laughed and said, "I'm not about to give you any money. I got a little old banty rooster that worries me to death because he's so vigrous. He don't get along with my chickens and you'd do me a favor if you'd take him. You might get fifty cents for him in town, some Saturday."

CHAPTER 5.

Bully

It took Lee and Sara and Pomp all three to round up the little bantam rooster and when Lee got a touch of his spurs he knew why Sara had said he was vicious.

The sun was going down back of the woods, throwing them into deep shadow, and when Lee said goodbye to old Sara, she said, "You're not a-scared to pass the graveyard, this time of evening, are you?" And she laughed as if this were a joke.

"No, ma'am," Lee said, now that he knew what to expect, "but I was kind of took back when I bumped into that stone angel in the storm."

Then old Sara smiled as if she were remembering something

pleasant, and she laughed softly to herself.

"Why, that little angel keeps me company," she said. "Since the big house burned down, long years ago, and my neighbors moved away, she's the best friend I've got."

Lee tucked the rooster firmly under his arm and whistled for Pomp. As they passed the burial-ground the little angel looked friendly and happy standing peacefully among the quiet gray stones. Lee's forgotten bucket lay at her feet with the berries tumbled and scattered. I reckon I'll have to leave them for the birds to pick, he thought. But he didn't feel too bad when he picked up the empty bucket. A rooster's worth a heap more than a mess of blackberries, he figured.

As if in answer to his thoughts, the long lonesome train whistle called through the dusk. "Ooooo-we-e-e-e-ooooo, ooooo-we-e-e-e-ooooo."

Lee broke into a gallop. That's the train a-heading back to Atlanta, he thought. And just as he reached the railroad cut it came around the bend.

"Ooooo-weeeeee-ooooo, ooooo-we-e-e-e-ooooo," called the whistle, and the big yellow eye of the engine's headlight sent a high shaft of light down the tracks. Then the soft summer dusk was filled with the roar of the train, and Lee could see sparks dancing in the smoke from the smokestack and the bright faces of the engineer and fireman in the glow from the open firebox, then rows and rows of square yellow lights from the coaches as they clacked by saying "At-LAN-ta, At-LAN-ta, At-LAN-ta."

Then suddenly they were gone and it was night and the two red taillights on the last car disappeared around the curve.

Lee held onto the little bantam rooster more tightly than before and said, "You'll bring me good luck one of these days and maybe I'll be a-going to Atlanta." And he hurried across the tracks and set out for home.

The little bantam rooster was "vigrous," all right. He set himself up as the champion of the chickens, first thing, and challenged everything in sight. He fought the old dominecker rooster until they were both bloody and bedraggled. He pecked Pomp on the tail when he lay dozing under the chinaberry tree and sent him loping off under the house for peace and quiet. He even challenged Lee's old Muscovy duck, who would usually chase away anything that moved.

"That little rooster is mighty feisty," Pa said. "Why, he's a fighter, little as he is."

And Ma said, "He keeps my chickens so riled up they're liable to stop laying."

"No wonder old Sara give him to you," Maggie Ellen said. "Can't nobody have any peace with him around. He's a trouble-maker."

"He's a bully all right," Lee agreed. "He's got the whole place a-scared of him."

After that everyone called the rooster Bully. The little bantam was pretty to look at, with his proud red comb and his blue-green tail feathers waving in the wind, and his bright orange ruff neat and combed-looking around his neck. When Bully stood in the sun with his head cocked to one side and one spurred, yellow foot lifted, ready to stroll across the sandy yard, he shone brightly, as if he were made of metal. Lee thought, I wouldn't take a pretty for that little old rooster.

Maggie Ellen and Lee tried a scheme for feeding Bully separately so the other chickens could eat in peace. Lee would coax Bully to follow him by sprinkling a little trail of corn around the side of the house while Maggie Ellen fed the chickens and ducks in the back. But Bully soon gobbled up his share and then sprinted

after the other chickens, grabbing up the best bites and calling the hens away from the big dominecker rooster to follow him.

Bully was always the first one up in the morning and the last to go to bed at night. Maggie Ellen said, "Bully won't sleep in the chicken house with the rest of the chickens. He's got to roost in the honeysuckle vines on the fence where he'll be the first to see the sun ever morning."

Lee loved the high, shrill voice of the little bantam rooster and he got to where he listened for it outside his window every morning. But his ma said, "I could wring that rooster's neck for crowing so close to the house. Why, he gets me up at the crack of dawn ever day."

CHAPTER 6.

The Picnic

One lazy summer day, when it was still enough to hear the bumblebees buzzing around the flower beds and the chickens making singing sounds under the chinaberry tree and Ruby Pearl crying sleepily inside the house, and Pomp snapping at flies on the porch, Lee said to Maggie Ellen, "That old swimming hole down by the trestle over Nickajack Creek sure would feel good along about now."

Maggie Ellen said, "I haven't been over that-a-way since last Fourth of July."

"It's mighty near the Fourth of July now," Lee said. "We could have us a picnic like we did last year."

Ma came out on the porch with Ruby Pearl half asleep on her shoulder. She sat down in her rocking chair and said, "If you all want to have a picnic you'll have to catch me some fryers. A picnic isn't no good without plenty of fried chicken and biscuits."

"I'll fix some hard-boiled eggs," said Maggie Ellen. "And Lee can go see if there's any ripe watermelons in the patch. They could be a-cooling in the spring till time for the picnic."

"Yonder comes Pa now," said Lee. "Let's ask him about the watermelons."

When Lee and Maggie Ellen told Pa about the picnic he liked the idea fine. "There's two watermelons bigger than Ruby Pearl, a-setting down there waiting for somebody to pick them. I thumped them to see if they was ripe just a little bit ago."

Lee helped his father fetch the watermelons from the patch and they put one of them in the spring and the other in the branch to cool.

Along about sundown Lee said, "Come on, Maggie Ellen, let's us go catch them chickens."

And their ma said, "I hope you'll catch that Bully. He'd be a heap more use in the frying pan than he is a-strutting around this place like he owned it."

But Pa said, "Why, he'd be so tough and stringy you couldn't eat him."

Lee thought, before I'd wring Bully's neck I'd starve to death. I'm not so sure I want to sell him, even.

Nickajack Creek was brown and swirling, with woods on

either side to keep it cool, and a smooth sandy beach between two great rocks for a picnic place. The railroad trestle rose up high across the creek, and blue sky showed through the open spaces between the crossties.

Lee and Maggie Ellen liked to wade upstream along the shallow bank of the creek as far as the trestle. Then they would swirl and tumble downstream with the current and bump down a little waterfall between two huge boulders until they reached the swimming hole. Here they would kick and splash each other and dive like frogs into the deep places and float on their backs and watch the sky through the leaves of overhanging branches.

Maggie Ellen said, "We ought to give Bubber a ride down the waterfall. Reckon he'd be a-scared?"

But Bubber wasn't, and he splashed and kicked and laughed while Lee and Maggie Ellen held onto him.

Pa picked up Ruby Pearl and held her over the shallow part of the creek dipping her fat feet into the water. She laughed and crowed happily, curling her pink toes each time they touched the water.

Ma called out, "Time you all dry off your underclothes and get dressed, we can eat."

Lee and Maggie Ellen and Bubber found a sunny place where their clothes would dry out and they laughed because their arms and legs and even their underwear were stained a reddish pink from the muddy water.

"Bubber looks like a Indian," Maggie Ellen said. "Why, he's

all over red from head to foot." They all laughed again.

When the chicken and biscuits and hard-boiled eggs and home-made pickle and red-ripe tomatoes were spread out, Pa said, "Which piece of chicken do you like, Lee?"

And Lee said, "The back, the breast and all the rest!" And they all laughed because this was what he always said.

Ma gave Bubber a drumstick and she let Ruby Pearl suck on a clean, smooth bone that just fitted her small fist.

Maggie Ellen said, "I got the wishbone! Let's make a wish."

She held it out to Lee and he crooked his little finger around one side of the Y-shaped bone while Maggie Ellen held the other side.

"I wisht we had some firecrackers for the Fourth of July," he said, but Maggie Ellen closed her eyes and wished for something to herself. They pulled and when the bone broke Lee held up the long side and sing-songed, "I got the wi-i-ish, I got the wi-i-ish!"

"You should of wished for something that could come true," Maggie Ellen said. "You expect firecrackers to drop out of the sky, right here and now?"

But before Lee could think of anything to say a low rumble came from the woods off in the distance and a train whistle blew from somewhere way off.

"Ooooo-weeeee-ooooo," it called. "Ooooo-weeeeeee-ooooo."

"The train's a-coming! The train's a-coming!" Lee shouted. "We can see her cross the trestle."

He and Maggie Ellen scrambled to their feet and Bubber ran after them crying, "Wait for me!"

They ran along the tangled creek bank, and waded where the bushes were thick. Maggie Ellen stopped and waited until Bubber could catch up and she helped him over the slippery rocks. But Lee didn't stop until he reached the trestle. Then he called back to Maggie Ellen and Bubber, "Hurry up, you all. She's a-coming round the bend."

The engine slowed and eased itself across the tall wooden bridge, pulling its coaches carefully and making echoes in the woods.

"Chuff - chuff - chuff - chuff - CHUFF - CHUFF - CHUFF - CHUFF - chuff - chuff - chuff - chuff - CHUFF - CHUFF - CHUFF - CHUFF," it chanted.

Lee and Maggie Ellen and Bubber waved and shouted and scrambled halfway up the slippery bank to see the engine better.

The engineer waved and smiled and then disappeared from view inside the cab. But as the engine passed over the last crosstie on the trestle he reappeared in the cab window, and leaning out, threw something—two somethings—long and red, which rolled and tumbled down the enbankment and landed at Lee's feet. Then he waved again and tooted his whistle, and before the children got over their surprise the train was gone.

"Pa! Pa!" Lee shouted, when the three of them had run breathlessly back to the picnic place. "The engineer throwed us something and they look like firecrackers. My wish come true! My wish come true!"

Pa examined the long red-papered cylinders. "Them's not firecrackers," he said. "Them's fusees. A railroad man always has to carry flares in case of danger. If there was trouble and he wanted to warn a oncoming train or one that was due to follow pretty soon, he'd set off the fusee. If somebody had of set off one of these things in time, my uncle Tom Henderson wouldn't of had no head-on collision."

"Well, it's the next best thing to a firecracker, seem like," Lee said. "Let's us set it off now."

"It wouldn't do no good until after dark," Pa said. "But time we eat the watermelons and get on back home it'll be dark enough."

That evening after every last bit of light had left the sky, Pa set off one of the fusees and stuck it into the ground by its sharp metal stem. The flare sputtered and burned and spread a vivid, fiery glow over the house and the chinaberry tree and the woods beyond, and lit up the faces of all the family until you could see them plain as day.

"Let's light the other one," Maggie Ellen said. "This is the best Fourth of July we ever had!"

But Lee said, "I'm a-going to save the other one till Christmas. It wouldn't be no fun at Christmas without firecrackers of some sort." And that night, before Lee went to bed, he put the fusee under his feather mattress where it would be safe and dry and where he wouldn't be tempted to set it off before Christmas time came.

All summer long, after that, Lee went to the railroad every chance he got. His pa said, "Ever time I turn my back that boy is gone. When that train whistle blows he hot-foots it over to Chinquapin Hill." And his ma said, "I can't get no work out of him at all. He's plumb crazy about trains."

Then Lee tried to get his work done faster so his folks wouldn't complain. But he never missed a chance to watch for the train. It seemed to Lee that the engineer, too, watched for him when he came around the bend. He always tooted his whistle in a certain sort of way. And as he passed the big rock where Lee was sitting he would slow the engine to a crawl and lean out the cab window and holler, "Hey there boy, how you been?"

But by the time Lee could holler "Hey" back, he was gone, with a little toot-toot from the whistle to say goodbye.

Once Lee took Maggie Ellen and Bubber with him to see the

train, and Bubber was so excited when he saw the big black engine that he jumped up and down and squealed with delight.

"When I grow up," Lee told Bubber, "I'll be the engineer and you can be the fireman."

"I wisht I could see the train at night, when she's a-heading back to Atlanta," Maggie Ellen said longingly. For Lee had told her of the wonderful sight he had seen that evening on his way home from Crazy Sara's.

"It sure was a pretty sight," Lee said, and he made up his mind that he would sell Bully the first chance he got, and, even if it took a year, he'd somehow get enough money to go to Atlanta on the train. Maybe he could even take Bubber and Maggie Ellen along too.

CHAPTER 7.

The Fight

When fall came and school started, Lee didn't have time to go to Chinquapin Hill to watch the train, except sometimes on a Saturday. But when school let out for the noon recess and he sat under the trees eating ham and biscuits and a sweet potato from his lunch pail, he'd listen for the train whistle. And when, every other day on its way to Chattanooga, he heard the whistle blowing loud and long through the railroad cut, he'd say to the children, "The engineer on that train is a friend of mine. He always blows that-a-way when he passes Chinquapin Hill, so I'll hear him."

One day Jaycee Cash heard Lee say this and he laughed aloud

and said, "It's no such of a thing. He's a-blowing for something on the tracks. Maybe one of Crazy Sara's wild hogs is ·a-butting his head against the cowcatcher."

Lee felt foolish in front of his friends. "Old Sara ain't crazy and her hogs ain't wild," he said to Jaycee rather sharply.

"She is, too, crazy," Jaycee insisted. "She put a spell on them old hogs and one of them like to wallowed Loy to death."

"Well, it was your nosy little old brothers that let her hogs out in the first place," Lee said. "Hogs is skittish around strangers sometimes."

Jaycee stood up and stuck out his chin. "Don't you call my brothers no names," he said. "And Crazy Sara is a old witch, too. We seen her and she's real snaggledy-toothed and she screeches at you ever time you pass."

"She was a-hollering at you to warn you about her hogs," Lee said, "and she was mad 'cause you let them a-loose."

Two of Jaycee's bigger brothers moved up behind him. Lee stood up and the other children in the yard gathered around.

"What we done to Crazy Sara wasn't nothing to what your old lop-eared hound done to our house." Jaycee said hotly. "He like to tore the place apart and we got whupped for it, too."

By now Lee was getting mad. "Pomp wasn't to blame," he hollered. "Your nosy little old brothers was the ones that drug him in the house with the pig and the chickens!"

Jaycee doubled up his fists and moved closer to Lee. "Well, you better keep your old dog tied up from now on," he screeched,

" 'cause my pa is a-going to shoot him if ever he catches him around our place again!"

Lee was so mad he couldn't see anything but Jaycee's face, which looked like a mask with slits for eyes and big grinning teeth and two red ears sticking out of straggly white hair.

"You lay a hand on my dog," he said, putting his face up to Jaycee's, "and I'll whup the tar out of you and your pa both."

Lee never knew who hit first. He felt his knuckles striking something hard and something harder hit him in the eye. And then he and Jaycee were rolling in the dirt with their legs locked and their fists flying. Lee half saw and half dreamed a circle of excited faces looking down on them and voices all about him yelling, "Move back!"—"Give 'em both room!"—"Knock the tar out of him!" But most of the faces looked like copies of Jaycee's face and most of the voices sounded like those of the Cash boys.

Lee could feel Jaycee's knees on his chest and he knew Jaycee was trying to pin his arms down and make him give up.

"You take back what you said about my brothers!" Jaycee was saying, still fighting to hold onto Lee's arms. But somehow Lee managed to free his legs, and pulling up his knees with a sudden jerk, he unseated Jaycee and rolled him over. He sat on Jaycee's chest and held onto his wrists while Jaycee flailed his arms and kicked like a steer.

"Make him say 'uncle'!" someone shouted, while Lee said, between short hard breaths, "You take back what you said about my dog!"

Jaycee kicked and squirmed, but Lee held on. "You take it back or I won't let you up."

"Aw, come on, Jaycee," someone called out. "It was a fair fight. You might as well admit you're licked!"

Jaycee swallowed hard and said, "I'll take it back this time, but you jest wait. I'll whup you good!"

Just then the school bell rang and both boys got up and dusted themselves off. The children clambered about Lee and said, "You fixed old Jaycee good, but we had to hold off his brothers. They was a-fixing to side in with him."

They all straggled toward the schoolhouse, with Jaycee and his brothers trudging along behind, jeering, "You better watch out. Next time we'll get you and your old dog both."

But Lee didn't even bother to answer.

When Lee came home from school that afternoon and he and Maggie Ellen told their folks about the fight, his pa said, "Well, I'll just vow! I thought Lee was a peaceable boy. But he don't take nothing off of nobody."

And Maggie Ellen said, "I bet Jaycee Cash won't say nothing about old Pomp again, long as he lives."

But Ma said, "If we don't do something about that black eye of Lee's he won't be in any kind of a fix to go to town, come Saturday."

Lee suddenly forgot about his black eye and his sore muscles, and all he could think was, here's my chance to sell Bully and make some money.

"I'll be all right by Saturday," he said. "Can't nothing stop me from going to town."

CHAPTER 8.

Bully
Goes to Town

When Saturday came Pa got Lee up extra early, and when the work was done he said, "I've got a load of wood all cut and ready to ride. If you'll help me load up the wagon, we'll get moving."

When the mule was harnessed and the wagon loaded, Lee said "Wait a minute while I catch Bully. I'm a-going to see can I sell him."

"I don't know who'd want that scrawny old rooster," Ma said. "But I'll sure be glad to get shut of him."

The day was crisp and cool, and the air was hazy and smelled of woodsmoke. The red, dusty road unwound ahead of the mule's floppy ears and from time to time Pa flicked the reins over his shiny rump and clucked to him and said, "Giddiyap, sir." But the mule only made ruffled sounds through his lips, shivered his short mane, and continued to clop lazily along. Pomp loped ahead, dipping into the roadside ditches that were bright with asters and goldenrod.

Pa said, "This time of year folks in town are glad to get a load of wood. It's getting kind of nippy at night."

"I hope somebody wants a rooster," Lee said. "But I sure hate to part with the little old fellow."

The mellow October sun shone down on Bully's bright head and on his feathers, making them glow red and gold and green and copper-colored, like the leaves on the trees.

"Coming into town, now in a minute," Pa said, clucking to the mule some more.

The road narrowed up ahead to a street arched with elms, and big, white houses with tall, smooth columns began to appear. Finally they came to the square in town where the red brick courthouse stood. Pa said, "Whoa there, boy," to the mule, and eased him into a space between the buggies and wagons that stood around the square. Lee jumped down and tied the reins to an elm tree, and his father fastened a feedbag of oats to the mule's nose, so he wouldn't strip the bark from the tree.

"Everbody and his brother is in town today, looks like," he said. "Court must be in session."

The courthouse steps were thick with men standing in groups talking, or sitting on their heels doing nothing, or watching the wagons and buggies coming in from the country. Children walked on the wall around the courthouse lawn or climbed on the statue of the Confederate soldier that stood with his musket straight beside him.

"Why don't you go on over to Fussell's store, and see can you sell your rooster," Pa said. "I want to pass the time of day with some of my friends."

Fussell's store was dim and smoky inside and filled with wonderful things. It smelled of cloth and leather and cheese and tobacco, and of wood burning in the pot-bellied stove, to take off the chill. Some women were buying calico for dresses and two children pressed their noses against the glass of the candy counter. Three or four men loafed about the stove, chewing tobacco and laughing at each other's jokes.

When Lee came in with Bully, someone said, "Where'd you get that rooster, boy?"

And Lee said, "He's for sale. I'm asking fifty cents for him."

Then someone laughed and said, "Won't nobody buy a bantam rooster. They got no meat on their bones."

But Lee set Bully on the counter and said to the storekeeper, "Reckon you might know of somebody that would want a rooster, Mr. Fussell?"

A big, red-faced man in overalls and a battered, wide-brimmed hat came up and clamped his hands over Bully, and held him up for everyone to see.

"Look at them spurs!" he said. "Why, this fellow would sure

be a winner in a cock-fight and that's the truth!"

Bully struggled and kicked his feet and made angry, squawking sounds in his throat, then suddenly got his wings free. Before the man could put him back on the counter, the little rooster had flapped out of his hands, leaving two long red scratches on the man's palms. Bully lit on the candy counter, but before Lee could grab him, he flew frantically to the back of the store and alighted on a horse collar hanging high on the wall with a "For Sale" sign on it.

Lee said, "Hey, mister, you scared my rooster half to death. I'll have a time a-catching him."

But the men around the stove were laughing and slapping their sides, and someone said, "He's for sale now, all right, but he's too high." And everybody laughed some more.

Mr. Fussell picked up a long-handled hoe and said to Lee, "You should of cropped his wings so he couldn't fly." Then he reached up with the hoe handle and tried to dislodge Bully. "Any time you bring a chicken to town you got to tie his feet together and cut his wings real short."

The little rooster looked down at him sideways and squawked angrily. Then, squatting low, and seeming to take aim, he made a long flapping dive from his perch and sailed across the store. Everybody ducked, but the red-faced man wasn't quick enough, and Bully knocked off his hat and then landed lightly on the edge of the big wooden cracked barrel. Quick as a flash, Lee grabbed the banty and tucked him firmly under his arm.

[65]

The men all laughed when the red-faced man stooped to pick up his hat, and one of them said, "If that little ole rooster had of flew a inch lower, you'd of come away without any ears."

Lee thought, Yes, and if you'd of kept those big hands offen him he never would of got away in the first place.

Just then Pa came in looking for Lee. "Somebody just told me Colonel Jake Moseley is a-looking for some wood," he said. "We'll have a bite to eat and then we'll go on over there."

Pa bought cheese and crackers and he bought himself some Brown's Mule tobacco. Then he fished a nickel out of the tobacco sack where he kept his change and gave it to Lee.

"You buy some licorice sticks and maybe some peppermint candy for Bubber and Maggie Ellen," he said.

Lee and his father sat in the wagon and ate the cheese and crackers. Lee said, "This tastes better than grits and red-eye gravy." And Pa agreed. Then he said, "How come you still got Bully? I thought you was a-raring to sell him."

Lee told what had happened in the store and then he said, "I'm not about to sell Bully if I have to tie his feet together and crop his wings."

Colonel Jake Moseley's house looks about as big as the courthouse, Lee thought, as they turned into the lane that ran along his side yard. The wagon wheels crunched over crisp fallen leaves, and Pomp bounded waist-deep in the bright, golden heaps that the sycamore trees and dropped against the fence.

Colonel Moseley was sitting in the sun on his wide, white-columned porch, and when he saw the wagon he waved his walking stick and hobbled down the steps and the red-brick path that led to his side gate.

"What are you asking for your wood?" he hollered.

Pa got down off the wagon. He and the colonel talked for a while and pretty soon Pa called out over his shoulder, "Lee, pull the wagon on down to the big gate yonder and we'll unload her."

Then Pa and Colonel Moseley walked down and opened the gate while Lee said "Giddiyap" to the mule and flipped the reins, calling out "Gee" when he wanted the mule to turn to the right.

The colonel pushed back the wide-brimmed army hat he was wearing, hooked his cane over his arm, and said, "Here, boy, I'll hold your rooster for you while you stack the wood."

When the wagon had been unloaded and the wood paid for, the colonel asked Lee, "What did you say your name was, boy?" And when Lee told him the colonel laughed until his mustache trembled and his blue eyes sparkled in his wide pink face. "Well I'll vow! I fought under General Lee for nigh onto four years, until I stopped a minnie ball with my leg, here." He patted his lame leg, and then, handing Bully over to Lee, reached deep into his pants pocket and pulled out a big silver dollar. "Take this for your trouble, boy. Anybody named for General Lee is a friend of mine."

That night Lee put his silver dollar in one of his father's old tobacco sacks and slipped it under his mattress along with his fusee. And for a long time after that he would get it out and look at it before he went to sleep at night, and he'd say to himself, "I wisht I had a heap more of these. I'd be a-heading for Atlanta right this minute."

CHAPTER 9.

House Afire!

When school let out for the Christmas holidays, Lee had more time to go over to Chinquapin Hill to watch the train. And the more he saw of it the more he wanted to ride on it. But he couldn't think of a way in the world to make any money.

"Can't nobody make money in the wintertime," his father said. "We'll be lucky if our cash money lasts till spring-planting time." Then he thought for a while and suddenly his brown eyes brightened with a new idea.

"I tell you what folks in town might buy, along about now," he said, "and that's Christmas trees. Why don't you and Aunt Susan's boy go see what you can find over in the piny woods?"

Lee didn't wait around to be persuaded. "If I can borrow your ax," he said, "I'll go fetch Matt and we'll go this afternoon."

The day was bright and cold and an icy wind blew in gusts across the yard. The chickens huddled together in the sun and the wind turned their feathers inside out. Bully's blue-green tail feathers fluttered like a flag, and the old Muscovy duck was almost lifted off her feet by the wind when she tried to follow Lee.

"Come on, Pomp," Lee called. "Here, boy." Pomp left his sheltered place beside the chimney and loped after him, glad of something to do. Lee shouldered his father's ax, pulled his red-knit stocking cap well down over his ears, and set out for Aunt Susan's.

Summer or winter, Aunt Susan's place always looked inviting to Lee, with its smooth, hard-packed yard and its large black iron wash pot outside waiting for washday. Now, it looked especially cozy, with shutters closed against the wind and smoke streaming from the chimney like a long, gray-blue horse's tail.

"Come on in," Aunt Susan called, when Lee hollered outside for Matt. The door opened against the wind and Matt's brown face appeared, his teeth showing white in a wide, glad grin. "Bring Pomp on in too and let him warm his foots," Aunt Susan laughed.

Lee and Pomp slipped inside and Matt fastened the door. The house was warm and shadowy and smelled of hickory smoke, and the light from the fire lit up three sleeping hound-dogs on the hearth. When they smelled Pomp they staggered to their feet, growling, but Aunt Susan said, "Hush your moufs! It's only Pomp and Lee."

"Where you going with that ax?" Matt wanted to know. "You fixing to chop down a tree?" And he doubled up with laughter and slapped his sides.

"I'm fixing to cut some Christmas trees," Lee said, warming his hands before the fire. And when Aunt Susan looked surprised he explained, "I'm a-going to sell them in town and see can I make enough money to go to Atlanta. If Matt can help me I'll split the money with him."

"I could sure use some cash money for Christmas," Matt said. "But it sure is a cold day to cut down trees."

"Who gonna haul the trees into town?" Aunt Susan asked sensibly. "Town folks expects you to cut 'em and haul 'em both."

"My Pa can haul all we can cut," Lee said.

Aunt Susan got up out of her rocking chair and stooped down in front of the fireplace and raked around in the ashes with her hands. "I got some good hot ash-cake 'bout done here," she said over her shoulder. "If you and Matt is going out in this wind you'll need something to stick to your ribs."

She dusted the ashes off the rough, hot pones of bread and filled them with chunks of freshly churned butter and poured buttermilk from a jug for the boys. And while the fire snapped and crackled and the flames waved in sudden gusts of wind from the chimney and the shutters at the windows slapped, Aunt Susan told about Atlanta. How it was before the war when her mother was a slave. About the great battle and the fire that you could see for fifty miles. How it was today.

Then she said suddenly, "You boys better git from here now, and cut your trees. It'll take heaps and piles of money to get to Atlanta nowadays."

Matt pulled an old felt hat down over his ears and turned up his coat collar against the cold and he and Lee struck out across fields that stretched in icy furrows towards the piny woods. Pomp **shot** out of Aunt Susan's house after them, but Matt's dogs decided to stay by the fire.

"Them old pines is too big for Christmas trees," Matt said, pointing to a stand of straight tall trees. The sun filtered through their green branches and made patterns on the ground, which was slippery with brown needles. The wind made a high icy song in the treetops.

"There's some little bitty pines up on the bank along the road," Lee said. "They ought to be real easy to chop down."

Lee and Matt took turns with the ax, and when they had a fragrant mound of the little pines, Matt said, "Your Pa gonna load these up this evening? It's near about sundown."

"We'll get them first thing tomorrow morning," Lee said. "Won't nobody bother them tonight."

They took a short cut through the woods and the sky began to fade to a cold wintry pink. "Hey, look!" Lee said, pointing to a large oak tree that stood apart on a little knoll. "Yonder's some mistletoe in the top of the tree. Let's us climb up and get it."

"I'm about froze," Matt said, beating himself with his arms and stamping his feet on the hard ground. "Let's us head for home before it gets dark."

But Lee looked up through the bare tangled branches of the tree to the cluster of green leaves and waxy cream-colored berries that nestled near the top. "It won't take long," he said, "if you'll give me a boost."

Matt shoved Lee up with his shoulder until he got a firm hold on the tree trunk and was able to claw and knee his way up to the lowest branches.

The wind sent heavy gusts through the woods, and Pomp
stirred up the leaves with his hind legs and followed a scent with
his nose.

The great oak loomed tall and dark in the dusk and pieces of
brittle twigs fell to the ground as Lee climbed. Suddenly his voice
rang out shrill and excited from above. "Come on up quick,
Matt!" he called. "Wait till you see what I see. Hurry!"

Matt forgot about the cold and shinnied up the tree like a
monkey, but he called up to Lee, "I don't want to sleep in no
tree tonight. I aim to get home before dark."

But Lee kept hollering, "Look over yonder where I'm a-point-
ing. Did you ever see the sun set in the east before?"

Matt climbed as high as he could get in the swaying tree and looked in the direction Lee was pointing. The sky beyond the trees glowed a deep red and even as the boys watched, black smoke billowed above the treetops.

"House afire!" Matt yelled, and without waiting for Lee he shinnied back down the tree, calling back, "That liable to be my house a-burning!"

Lee followed, forgetting the cold, and make a hard, pounding drop from the lowest limb of the tree. Scrambling among the leaves for his ax, he called out, "Hey, wait for me!" and "Here, Pomp!" all in the same breath.

Matt ran ahead through the woods and Lee and Pomp followed. But when Matt reached the pasture beyond, he slowed down.

"It ain't your house or mine, either one," he said, when Lee had caught up. "It's over in the direction of Chinquapin Hill."

"Well then, it's old Sara's or the Cashes' house, one," Lee said. "Let's us go see."

Now, through a straggle of woods beyond the pasture, the sky burned a wild angry red. Flames and sparks leaped above the treetops, and the wind brought the acrid smell of smoke across the meadow.

"It's the Cash place!" Lee cried. "It's too close for Crazy Sara's." And they started to run.

When they reached the Cash place, all that was left of the house was a blackened skeleton filled with flames. Lee's heart jumped. What if some of them was still in there? he thought. What if they couldn't get out?

Then, with relief, he saw the Cashes all huddled in a group in the yard. The smallest children were crying, and Mrs. Cash, holding a baby in her arms, was going about among her children calling, "You there, Jaycee? Where's Roy and Loy?" and "Addie Myra, you help me count and see if they's all here."

Automatically Lee began to count too, and he was relieved when he reached number ten. He recognized Jaycee all black with soot, holding an iron frying pan in his hand. Lee ran up to him and said, "Wasn't nobody left inside, was there, Jaycee?"

Jaycee began to talk furiously, choking back sobs and wiping his nose with a grimy fist. "It was my fault," he said. "I went off and left Stonewall Jackson and Roy and Loy while my folks was away, and they was a-playing Yankee prisoner again. That fool pig knocked a chunk of wood out of the fireplace and set the house on fire."

"It wasn't your fault," said Lee. "They should a-knowed better after last time."

"I got most all the ducks and chickens out of the house, 'cept maybe one. Roy and Loy and Stonewall Jackson pushed the pig out and then they run. Onlyest thing I could save was my ma's spider." He held up the iron frying pan and looked at it sorrowfully. Then he heaved another great sob and said, "I'm a-gonna get whupped, sure."

About that time the roof fell in with a crash and the flames fanned out furiously in the wind. Mr. Cash came pounding across the yard from somewhere in the back and called to his boys, "Come help me get the critters out of the barn. If this wind keeps up hit'll be the next thing to go."

Lee and Matt started to follow, when suddenly someone ran

up from behind them and grabbed the ax out of Lee's hand. It was Pa. "We'll be a-needing this," he called back over his shoulder. "If the wind shifts won't be nothing left of the barn. You stay here, Lee, and see can you help Mrs. Cash."

"If we had a bucket," Lee said, "we could haul some water up from the branch."

"Ain't no use," Matt said. "That old house is long gone."

They went over to where Mrs. Cash and the children stood huddled together. Lee tried to think of something to say, but when Mrs. Cash saw him she spoke calmly. "We sure are lucky. Didn't a hair on our heads get hurt." Then she turned and looked proudly at Jaycee. "You know what that boy of mine done? He run back in the house and saved my spider. Why, I wouldn't a-had a pan to cook in if he hadn't a-done that!"

About that time Aunt Susan ran up, panting and reaching out her arms for one of the smaller children.

"I seed the flames all the way from my house and I come to get some of these young-uns in out of the cold. I could take many as you want me to and keep 'em long as you like."

Then it seemed that everybody from miles around was there. Old man Zack rumbled up in his wagon, hopped down excitedly and tied his mule to a tree by the road.

"Where's all the menfolks at?" he hollered to Lee as he hobbled across the yard. But before Lee could answer he had headed for the barn, calling back over his shoulder, "Reckon they'll be needing another hand."

[79]

The heat from the fire was terrific. Matt said, "Minute ago I was a-freezing and now I'm roasting hot."

Suddenly, as if there were nothing left for the hungry flames to feed on, the fire settled to a slow, crackling burn.

"Hey, look!" Lee shouted. "The wind's dying down!" For the first time they saw that the flames were licking straight up, lighting the naked blackened chimney which was all that was left of the Cashes' home.

"I reckon we're the luckiest people alive," Mrs. Cash said, huddling the smaller children up closer to Aunt Susan. "Another minute and we'd of been without a barn."

The men and boys came up, looking relieved and talking excitedly. "We figured it had to be your place," old man Zack was saying to Mr. Cash. "We seed the flames clean over to the grist mill." Then he turned to Mrs. Cash and said, "My old lady made me bring some quilts along in the wagon for you all to wrap up in. She told me to bring back as many of you as wanted to stay at our place."

Just then a lantern came bobbing along over the path from Chinquapin Hill. Before anyone could see who it was, Crazy Sara's high, quavery voice called out, "I seen the glow in the sky from 'way over beyond the burying-ground and I come to see what I could do for you all."

And before the last of the embers had died out, the Cash family was settled for as long as it would take to rebuild their home.

Aunt Susan and Matt took the smaller children because Aunt

Susan loved the best in the world to hear little bitty feet running about her house. Crazy Sara took the big girls because she was lonesome and liked to have woman-talk around her place. Mr. and Mrs. Cash and the baby and the big boys went with old man Zack because there was a heap of room at his house and, besides, he could use some help at the mill.

Roy and Loy and Stonewall Jackson and Jaycee went with Lee and his pa because they were all friends, anyway, and Christmas would be more fun with a bunch of boys around.

That night, with pallets and quilts spread to sleep on, and the fire warm and cozy and the night outside still and cold, everybody talked until long past bedtime about the fire and how it happened. Lee went to sleep with a warm feeling inside him, and he was somehow very happy.

CHAPTER 10.

The Head-on Collision

Long after the Cashes had moved into their new house which the neighbors had helped to build, and when the days had settled into a long, cold wait for spring, the excitement of the fire was relived by everyone; nothing seemed quite so interesting to talk about.

"Me and Matt rolls around like marbles now, in our empty house," Aunt Susan said. "I sure misses them little old Cash young-uns. I loved them like they was my very own."

Crazy Sara said, "They's nothing like having girls around the house to keep things prettied up." And then she added brightly, "You know, Addie Myra's about learned to play my organ. Why, she still comes over mighty near ever day, and we have a real nice concert together."

"I thought I was a-getting old until I had them Cash boys around to help," old man Zack said. "Why they plumb took over my grist mill." Then he laughed until he doubled over, and said, "I'm a-going to have me some company next time I go coon hunting, too. Them boys gets along good with my old coon dog."

Mrs. Cash said, "Lee and Matt give me the money to buy me some cooking pots and some dishes. They claimed they sold some Christmas trees in town and made four dollars on them."

Jaycee said to Lee, "You must a-had a heap of money hid out. Where did you get that silver dollar to buy all them firecrackers and marbles for me and Roy and Loy and Stonewall Jackson?" But Lee didn't tell Jaycee that ever since the Cash kids had been there, he hadn't been able to find his fusee. And Christmas wouldn't have been Christmas without firecrackers.

But Ma said, "I like to lost my mind with them twins and Stonewall Jackson. Ever time I turned my back they had Bully or that old Muscovy duck hid out somewhere in my house. Why, if I hadn't watched out, I reckon they'd of brought in the pigs, too."

Then Pa said, "Well, ever how much trouble them least Cash kids was, Jaycee made up for it on Christmas day when he brought over that little old banty hen that lost her mate in the fire." And he chuckled softly as he thought it over. "Why, Bully's tame as a dove now that he's got him a wife."

After Lee had spent his silver dollar and the Christmas tree money he gave up any idea of going to Atlanta. But when the Cashes had left and the house was back in order, he did find his fusee hidden among the quilts where the twins had slept. Then he remembered his friend, the engineer, and thought to himself, I can still watch the train, even if I can't ride on it. And he started going again to Chinquapin Hill.

On long winter evenings, when it was raining or sleeting outside and the wind was throwing itself against the doors and windows like an angry giant, and the train whistle moaned lonesomely in the night, Lee would coax his father to sing the railroad songs he knew and tell about his uncle Tom Henderson's head-on collision.

Pa would take down his fiddle from the mantelpiece and scrape his fiddle bow across the strings a few times to get in tune, and pat his foot, and sing, in his deep voice that had a tremble in it.

> "'Twas a-rainin' and a-sleetin' and the night was inky black
> And Uncle Tommy Henderson was speedin' down the track.
> With his hand upon the throttle and his eye upon the rail
> Uncle Tommy said, 'The road ahead is black as a
>   widow's veil.' "

And then he'd say, "Why, it was on a night sort of like this one, a-raining and a-blowing and as dark as a stack of black cats. And number 9, my uncle Tom Henderson's train, was a-heading south; number 2, the passenger train from Atlanta, was a-heading north, on the same track."

"Why didn't someone warn your uncle Tom about the other train?" Maggie Ellen wanted to know.

Then Pa would draw a picture in the ashes on the hearth with a stick, to show how it was, and he'd say, "Number 2 was supposed to wait in the siding, like here." And he'd point to a little curve of track that lay along the side of the track that he had drawn. "But somebody had fooled with the switch and

Number 2 went lickety-split right down the same track that Number 9 was on coming south."

"How come somebody didn't set off a fusee?" Lee asked. "I thought they was supposed to be used in time of danger."

"They are," replied Pa. "But it was a-raining and a-sleeting and didn't nobody know what had happened until it was too late. Uncle Tom looked up and saw this great old big headlight a-coming down the tracks, closer and closer, and a-getting bigger and bigger. All he had time to do was slam on the brakes and pull the whistle and holler, 'Jump!' to his fireman. And then they hit, BAM!"

Lee and Maggie Ellen and Bubber sat stiff and breathless, afraid their father wouldn't go on. Even Ma stopped her rocking, and Pomp raised up his head to see what was the matter.

Then Pa's voice got deeper and his eyes shone in the firelight, remembering.

"When them two engines locked horns you could a-heard it all the way across Sugar Valley, like the world was a-coming to an end. And the coaches all crashed into each other and splintered up like match boxes. You could hear folks a-hollering for help, and the engines was just two big mountains of twisted steel where the boilers had exploded when they hit."

"Was many folks kilt?" Maggie Ellen asked, shivering, and her voice hardly louder than a whisper.

"A heap of folks was hurt," her father replied. "But my uncle Tom saved the other engineer and fireman by taking time to blow his whistle. That give them time to jump. And I reckon if he hadn't a-done that it might a-been a heap worse."

Then, because he knew this was what they wanted to hear most, Pa continued, "Me and my daddy got there right soon after it happened and we helped pull folks out of the wreckage. Nobody ever did know for sure how many folks was on them two trains. But everbody in the county come and helped, seem like. It took two days to clear the track, with a wrecker from Chattanooga and another one from Atlanta."

"Tell what happened to your uncle Tom," Maggie Ellen said, although she had heard the story over and over.

"Why, old uncle Tom hit on a milepost when he jumped and broke his right arm and right ankle. But his fireman rolled down the embankment on the other side of the engine and he got off without a scratch!"

Ma said, "I wouldn't want no boy of mine to be a railroad engineer. It's too dangerous."

"Why, my uncle Tom went right back to railroading soon's he got well," Pa said. "Some folks is just borned engineers."

"I'm a-going to be an engineer when I grow up," Lee said, "even if it is dangerous."

When he went to bed, and before he fell asleep, Lee would picture his engineer friend on engine 1326 coming down the dark tracks, on just such a night as this, heading into some unseen danger. And Lee would picture himself running along the tracks in the rain and setting off his fusee to save his friend.

CHAPTER 11.

Rain, Rain, Rain

"Well, look a-there!" Ma said one morning, glancing out the window at her flower bed along the fence. "My jonniquills is all up and fixing to bloom."

Lee pulled on his jeans and shirt and ran out into the yard. The day was gray and chilly, but the new green blades of his mother's jonquils stood bravely waving fat buds ready to burst. Bully and his little banty wife picked and scratched under the chinaberry tree and the old Muscovy duck came up, bobbing her neck and waggling her tail. The ducks and chickens strolled up to the kitchen door to be fed, and Pomp bounded down off the back porch, scattering them and barking to make them squawk.

Pa came out and stood in the doorway and sniffed the cool, damp air. "Looks like we're a-going to have a early spring," he said. "I'm glad I've got a fella big enough to be some help with the plowing."

Lee was glad there was work to be done after the long cold months of sitting before the fire. He loved to feel the tug and pull of his father's plow behind the mule's big back. He loved making the deep red furrows in curving rows across the field. He loved dropping seed into the moist, loose earth and watching for the first green sprouts to appear like lines of little soldiers.

"I aim to help you a heap this year," he said, his long legs restless and ready to run. "I could plow that whole field and never know the difference."

His father laughed. "First time that old train whistle blows you'll be long gone over to Chinquapin Hill," he said.

"I'm not studying about going to watch no train," Lee said, "let alone go to Atlanta."

But he heard the train whistle calling wherever he was or whatever he was doing.

"Oooo-weeeeee-oooooo," it called, "oooooo-weeeee-ooooo."

And when it chuffed across the trestle over Nickajack Creek it still seemed to say, "CHATTA-noo-ga, CHAT-ta-nooga, CHAT-a-nooga, CHAT-ta-nooga." Or, on the return run, "At-LAN-ta, At-LAN-ta, At-LAN-ta."

But the warm weather was long in coming, and even after the jonquils had burst into bloom and lit up the yard like a patch of yellow sunshine, a cold snap came.

"I reckon this is the last cold spell before Easter," Pa said. "The weather don't never settle down good till Easter's come and gone."

One morning Ma exclaimed, "Well, I wish you'd look a-there! My jonniquills is all in bloom and it a-snowing!"

Lee and Maggie Ellen and Bubber all dashed to the window. They couldn't believe their eyes when they saw the snowy flakes fluttering past and settling into the deep yellow cups of the jonquils.

Rain and sleet and ice came often in the winter, but snow was somewhat rare, and even when it did come, it never wanted to stay.

"Maybe if we hurry, we can make us a snowman before the snow melts," Maggie Ellen said. But soon the snow was melted under a tender warm sun, and the jonquils were laughing as if nothing had happened, while the roof of the house dripped slow steady tears where the snow had been.

Then it began to rain. It rained and it rained and it rained. The yard ran in gullies, the lane was pink and slippery, and the road was deep in red mud.

"I'm a-going to lose my mind," Ma said, "if you all don't stop a-tracking that old red clay into my house."

"We're liable to have a flood, if this keeps up," Pa said, "and with it a-thawing up around north Georgia, the rivers is going to be all swolled up over their banks."

"The branch is way up over the bank now," Lee said. "I bet old Nickajack Creek is a-fixing to flood." And he made up his mind that if it ever stopped raining long enough he'd go over there and see for himself.

"Can't nobody do any work·in weather like this," Pa said. "The porch is a-leaking and the barn's a-leaking and the rain won't let up long enough to fix them."

But one afternoon the rain did stop for a while and the sun came out warm and golden over the dripping trees and the drenched fields and fences. Lee said, "I'm a-going over and take a look at Nickajack Creek." And he called Pomp and they set off together.

Mud oozed between Lee's toes as he walked along the road and he had to roll up his pants where the puddles were deep. The Cashes' house shone raw and new, with its unpainted pine boards wet with the rain. Lee would have liked to stop in and ask Jaycee to go with him, but he thought, If I hang around there it's liable to set in and rain some more.

The woods on Chinquapin Hill were dripping in a steady patter, patter, and the sun lit the new young leaves that sparkled with droplets of water.

Lee went to the big rock over at the railroad cut, but Pomp ran free through the woods, shaking showers out of all the bushes.

Lee knew it wasn't time for the train to pass, but he sat on the rock anyway and peered up and down the tracks. The rain sure

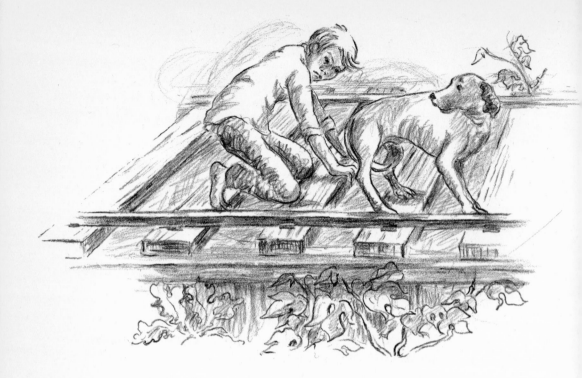

washed out the bank a heap, he thought to himself. From where he sat on the rock he could see deep gullies in the cut, and beside the rock, where the honeysuckle vines didn't grow, the clay had washed down until the crossties were stained a bright red-orange.

One more rain like this one, Lee thought, and this old rock might come a-loose. He jiggled it a little and imagined that it moved.

He noticed that the sun had disappeared again under the clouds, so he whistled for Pomp and started walking the long silvery railroad tracks toward the creek.

RAIN, RAIN, RAIN!

Before he got to the trestle he could hear the rush and gurgle of Nickajack Creek, and when he saw it at last he almost cried out with surprise. Its swirling, muddy water was deep red from the clay it had washed from faraway fields, and its crest was over halfway up the bank under the trestle. The little beach where Lee's family had spent the Fourth of July was not to be seen, and the big rocks where the children had ridden the little waterfall had disappeared under angry whirlpools of water. Leaves and sticks and broken tree branches floated in the current, turning and whirling and catching along the banks of the stream.

Lee ventured across the trestle, stepping cautiously along on the crossties and going carefully on his hands and knees when the swirling water in the gaps below made him feel dizzy. He got almost to the middle of the trestle when he thought, I better turn around. I might not make it back before dark. For even then the sky was gray and gloomy and the rain was starting up again.

Suddenly Lee heard a loud echoing crash from the cut along Chinquapin Hill. A chill of fear ran down his spine and as soon as his feet left the last crosstie of the trestle he began to run down the tracks, leaping over the ties, two at a time. And up ahead, around the curve he saw a great gray shape lying across the tracks. He knew at once what had happened.

"The big rock's come a-loose from the bank!" he cried out loud, but the pelting rain drowned out his voice.

A hundred thoughts a minute raced through Lee's mind as

he stood looking at the huge stone; he tried senselessly to make it budge. What if the train was to come along? How could he stop it? How long before the train for Atlanta was due? What would happen if he couldn't get help?

Then his head cleared, and he began to think. It wasn't quite sundown, even though you couldn't tell from the sky. The train usually came along about dark, and sometimes later since the rains had begun. If he hurried he could get home and tell Pa and get back with his fusee and set it off in time to stop the train before it got across the trestle.

But what if he couldn't make it? He had lost track of the days lately, and this might be the day for the engineer on Number 1326 to be going to Atlanta. I've got to make it! he thought. And he began to run.

CHAPTER 12.

Fusee to the Rescue

Somehow, through the driving rain and the darkening woods and the short-cuts over slippery clay banks and ankle-deep, muddy furrows, Lee reached home. He didn't have time to answer his mother when she called, "Get out of my house with all that mud!"

He ran straight to his bed and fumbled for the fusee under the mattress. Snatching off a pillow-case, he wrapped the fusee in it to keep it dry, and ran out again calling, "Tell Pa to hurry! There's a rock on the tracks at Chinquapin Hill, and it's liable to wreck the train!"

When Lee got back to the place where the rock had fallen, he knew what he had to do. His breath was coming in painful gasps, and he was soaked through to the skin, but his head was clear, and he said to himself, "I'll have to cross the trestle to set off the signal. If I don't, there won't be time enough for the train to stop."

Lee didn't know how frightened he was until long after it was over. He groped and crawled and felt his way across the black, open bridge, and was glad he couldn't see the dark swirling waters of Nickajack Creek below. He didn't hear the moan of the train whistle until he was almost across the trestle, and then, way up ahead, he saw the great headlight coming around the curve.

Somehow he managed to set off the fusee and stab it into the ground, and as it flared brilliantly, he ran down the tracks toward the train. He jumped from the track as the train came to a squealing grinding clanging stop. Then he heard a great hissing of steam and the pad of running feet toward him, and suddenly the face of his friend, the engineer, looked down on him.

"Well, I'll just vow!" the engineer exclaimed, when he saw Lee. "Was it you set off that fusee? If this is a joke of some kind, I'll tan your hide!"

Lee pointed up ahead. "Big rock on the track!" he gasped. "The bank's plumb washed away, other side of the trestle."

Lee led the way across the trestle, sure-footed this time, in the light from the fusee. The engineer and fireman and the

conductor, and even some of the passengers, trooped along after him, exclaiming, "That young 'un sure had a lot of nerve crossing the trestle on a night like this," and, "How come you to notice the washout, boy?" and, "Where did you get a-holt of a fusee, anyway? They don't grow on trees."

Then Lee and the engineer laughed because they both knew the story. "I saved out one of them fusees you give me for the Fourth of July," Lee said, "and it sure come in handy tonight."

When they got to the place where the rock had fallen, they were surprised to find Pa already there, with the mule, and a long, strong chain, and some rope. Mr. Cash was there too, holding a lantern, and all the Cash boys were with them standing around telling Pa how to harness the mule up to the rock so he could pull it off the track.

Then Pa and the engineer and fireman and Mr. Cash stood about studying the situation, and after talking things over, decided just how to get the chain around the rock and harness it to the mule. Finally, amid shouts of "Giddiyap there, boy!" and "Heave!" and "All together, now!" the mule strained and stumbled and the rock came free.

Shouts and laughter rang out in the night, and the engineer said to Pa, "Where's that boy of yours? If it hadn't been for him we'd a-been smashed to smithereens!" Lee hung back, but the engineer grabbed his hand in a hard grip and said, "Boy, I'll not forget this night if I live to be a hundred!"

When the train had finally crept across the trestle and the

two red tail-lights had disappeared around the curve, Pa said to Lee, "I'm a-going to ride you home on the mule, Lee. You must be plumb wore out."

Lee fell asleep almost before he had sunk into the soft nest of his feather bed and pulled the patchwork quilt up around his head. He didn't even hear his pa say proudly, "If my uncle Tom had of had a boy like Lee on the lookout for him he wouldn't of never had no head-on collision."

CHAPTER 13.

Lee Gets a Letter

The next day and the next and the next, his mother said, "I'm not a-going to let you go to school with that cough. Why, you like to caught your death of cold the other night." She kept him in bed with a mustard plaster on his chest and a warm flat-iron at his feet to sweat out the cold.

At first Lee liked staying at home with nothing to do but talk over the exciting events of that black, rainy night. But when the weather cleared at last and the air was filled with warmth and sweetness and the songs of birds, he thought he couldn't stay in the house another minute and he longed for a chance to go back to Chinquapin Hill. .

"I reckon the sun would do you good," his mother said when she saw how restless Lee was. "But it won't hurt you none to stay out of school one more day."

Lee knew his mother meant for him to stay around home, but this was his only chance to go to the railroad cut, and without saying a word to anyone he slipped away.

The embankment didn't look the same with the rock washed away, and there was no longer a good place to sit. So Lee followed the little path that wound its way down to the tracks and on across to Crazy Sara's. Almost before he got there, the whistle blew long and loud, and the train loomed into view around the curve. For one breathtaking moment, Lee stood in the middle of the tracks and waved, then jumped back as the train tooted again, far down the tracks. Lee stood watching, ready to wave again as it passed. But instead, the train began to slow down, and as it drew closer, the engine came to a full panting stop.

"Hey there, boy!" the engineer called down from his lofty perch. "How'd you like a ride on the engine?"

For a minute Lee stood in open-mouthed astonishment, then he leaped for the gangway between the engine and tender and climbed the high narrow iron steps.

The engineer and fireman were both laughing and talking at the same time. They hollered above the noise of the engine as it lurched and steamed and chuffed into motion.

"Come over here and work the firebox for me while I shovel

in some coal," shouted the fireman, and he showed Lee how to step on the treadle that opened the firebox door.

Lee braced himself against the swaying and jerking of the engine and watched in wonder as the fireman scooped shovels of coal from the tender and tossed them into the banked-up fire. The fireman laughed at Lee and his white teeth gleamed in his sweating black face.

The engineer reached over and pulled at Lee's arm. "Come over here, boy, and I'll let you run the train," he hollered. "If it hadn't of been for you we wouldn't have no engine."

Lee clambered over to the engineer's seat and his friend said, "Here's the throttle, and yonder's the whistle. Go to it!"

Lee grasped the throttle while the engineer guided his hand. A thrill of excitement ran through him as he felt the speeding wheels under the engine, and the hot smoky spark-filled breeze that lifted his hair. The tracks ahead melted like magic and the tree-topped scallops of Chinquapin Hill flashed by, giving back echoes of their noise. Then the woods fell away and the trestle appeared, high and naked and narrow.

"I'll take her across the creek," the engineer shouted. "You can sit by the window and look down."

Lee looked, and it seemed to him there was nothing under the engine but the sound of the wheels click-clacking the rails over endless crossties, and, far below, the muddy curling waters of Nickajack Creek.

"Reckon this old trestle is a-going to hold up?" he called out

over the chuff and clang of the engine. But he felt a little foolish
for asking.

"You wasn't a-scared to cross it alone at night, was you?" the
engineer laughed, and the fireman laughed with him. "I reckon
it'll hold up one more time, if we take it easy."

Then the engineer said, "When we get around the bend you
come over here and blow the whistle, two longs and two shorts.
There's a schoolhouse over yonder a piece and I always blow for
a friend of mine that might be a-listening out for it."

For the first time Lee realized that the schoolhouse showed
itself for one fleeting moment, through a gap in the hills. He
pulled the whistle cord and fell back laughing each time the
valve opened up in a voice loud enough to drown out every
other sound. Lee wished he could go on forever, speeding down
the tracks and pulling the whistle all the way. But the engineer
began slowing the train down, and he handed Lee a piece of
clean cotton waste.

"Wipe some of that smoke and grease off your hands," he
said. "I got something I want to give you before I let you off."
He fished around in the pocket of his overall jacket, pulled out
a smudged white envelope, and handed it to Lee.

"Don't lose this," he said. "It's a letter from the Superintendent of the railroad, and there's something else besides."

The train stopped and Lee just had time to reach out and take
the letter and say "Much obliged" before he clambered down
the gangway. He turned to wave.

"Now, you get on to school," the engineer hollered. "If you take the short-cut through the woods yonder, you might get there in time for recess."

Before the last coach clicked by, Lee had the letter open and was spelling out the neat typewritten words to find out what the little folded blue paper clipped to the top of the letter meant.

"Dear Lee," the letter said. "The Southern Railroad deeply appreciates your act of courage in stopping Engine 1326 on the night of . . ." There was more, but Lee skipped to the last paragraph. "We are enclosing herewith a pass which will allow you and your family to ride free on any train of the Southern Railroad for one year."

Lee couldn't believe the words he read, and he spelled them out to himself over and over. Then he looked at the blue folded ticket with the letters S.R. on it, for Southern Railroad, with his own name neatly typed on the face of it and the tall spidery scrawl of the superintendent's signature.

At last he put the letter away, and turning toward the path in the woods, he began to hurry in the direction of the schoolhouse. If he could get there before recess was over he could show the letter to his friends.

Then Lee thought of his mother and how mad she'd be when she found out he had slipped off. "Maybe she'll forget when I show her the letter," he said to himself. Maybe me and Pa and Maggie Ellen can talk her into going to Atlanta on the train and even taking Bubber and Ruby Pearl!

And he ran along the path with the sound of the train whistle still singing in his ears.